CW00551560

The
Quartet

Published with the financial support of the Ministère de la Communauté française de la Belgique, and the French Ministry for Foreign Affairs, as part of the Burgess programme headed for the French Embassy in London by the Institut Français du Royaume-Uni.

The
Quartet

FRANÇOIS EMMANUEL

Translated from the French by Euan Cameron

review

Copyright © 2000 Editions Stock

English translation © 2001 Euan Cameron

The right of François Emmanuel to be identified as the Author
of the Work has been asserted by him in accordance with the
Copyright, Designs and Patents Act 1988.

First published in 2001 by REVIEW

An imprint of Headline Book Publishing

10 9 8 7 6 5 4 3 2 1

All rights reserved. No part of this publication may be
reproduced, stored in a retrieval system, or transmitted,
in any form or by any means without the prior written
permission of the publisher, nor be otherwise circulated
in any form of binding or cover other than that in which
it is published and without a similar condition being
imposed on the subsequent purchaser.

All characters in this publication are fictitious
and any resemblance to real persons, living or dead,
is purely coincidental.

British Library Cataloguing in Publication Data

Emmanuel, Francois
The quartet
I.Title
843.9'14[F]

ISBN 0 7472 7070 8

Typeset by Letterpart Limited, Reigate, Surrey

Printed and bound in Great Britain by Clays Ltd, St Ives plc

Headline Book Publishing
A division of Hodder Headline
338 Euston Road
London NW1 3BH

www.reviewbooks.co.uk
www.hodderheadline.com

'In a dark time the eye begins to see'

Theodore Roethke

For seven years I was employed by a multi-national firm which I shall refer to by the name of SC Farb. This organisation, which was of German origin, owned an important subsidiary company in a mining town in north-eastern France. I was employed there as a psychologist in what was known as the human resources department. My job had a dual function: selection of personnel, and coordinating seminars for the members of staff. I see no point in expanding further on the nature of these seminars: they were inspired by the new business culture that places staff motivation at the core of

1

production planning. The methods used there were based indiscriminately on role play, experience of group dynamics, and even on ancient oriental techniques in which people were encouraged to exceed their personal limitations. Since we were living, by definition, in a hostile environment, warlike metaphors played an important part, and my task was to awaken the natural aggressiveness of those who were participating in order to make them more involved, more efficient, and thus, in the long run, more productive. In these seminars I have seen mature men weep like little boys, and I have persevered with them until they were able to lift up their heads again and could get back to work with that glint of false victory in their eyes. Now I see that glint is just like a look of deep despair. Without batting an eyelid, I have witnessed brutal confessions and outbursts of crazed violence. It was part of my job to channel all this towards the sole objective assigned to me: to make soldiers, captains of industry and competitive juniors out of these executives, so that this subsidiary of SC Farb should once more become the flourishing concern it had been in former days.

It should be said that the company was just recovering from an extremely difficult period. A plan for restructuring had been set up four years earlier that entailed the closure of a production line and a reduction in staff numbers from 2,500 to 1,600. Indirectly, I had been implicated in this consolidation, having been requested by management to develop certain criteria for the evaluation process other than those of age or length of service. But I can't yet speak about my part in this. There is a sequence to the events of this story that has less to do with chronological facts than with the dreadful, slow unfolding of my own awareness. The person in charge of this reorganisation, and the managing director of the French subsidiary, was a man called Mathias Just. I had had a number of what one might call organic contacts with him (staff meetings, exchanges of memoranda), but I only knew him through the somewhat aloof image of himself he maintained among all his employees: that of the secretive executive, a rather fraught and touchy sort of man, who was a creature of dogma and duty, and a slave to work. Any decision he made was irrevocable, even if it was preceded by a show of consultation. After the restructuring, the head office in Germany had sent someone by the name of Karl Rose, the nature of whose job was rather vague, to assist him: he was deputy managing director, and he was particularly concerned with staff matters. Rumours were rife as to the relationship between the two men, even though they called themselves friends and never failed to present themselves as supportive colleagues whose opinions never differed. It should be said that in certain respects Karl Rose seemed to be the exact opposite of Mathias Just. He was an attractive man in his forties with an easy, approachable manner: he was on familiar terms with his secretaries, and liked to mix with the staff, many of whom he was on first-name terms with. This reassuring exterior concealed a man who was highly skilled in personal relationships, a crafty speculator who was pleasantly cynical and who seemed to move his pieces forward one by one in a game whose essential purpose remained hidden.

When Karl Rose summoned me personally to his office one day in November 19--, I had a foreboding that the meeting would not be straightforward. It had snowed

heavily that day, unusually early for the sea-
son. Because of various delays caused by the
snow, I had had to postpone my morning
meetings. Rose showered me with compli-
ments as he greeted me, saying that he
valued my dynamism, and he congratulated
me for having introduced into my seminars
this 'new concept of business relationships'
which was beginning to produce results.
Having established this, he requested his
secretaries not to disturb him on any
account and he demanded complete confidentiality for what he was about to discuss
with me. His expression suddenly grim, he
said that he had been ordered by head
office to apprise me of a worrying problem.
It was a serious matter since it concerned
Mathias Just himself. (He pronounced the
name in the German way: Iust.) Before pro-
ceeding further, he enquired about the
nature of my relationship with the managing
director. I replied that it was strictly professional, that I did not know the man in any

private capacity, and that we met rarely, at office meetings. Otherwise, we greeted each other courteously without ever exchanging more than casual remarks. My answer approximated to the truth. 'I mentioned confidentiality,' said Rose, 'because as a psychologist you are bound to be aware of the responsibility this word implies. Let me be perfectly clear: it is with you alone that I wish to share *our* concerns.' He then told me about a series of suspicions relating to what one was bound to describe as Just's mental health. These suspicions were left somewhat vague, unless it was that he was being deliberately unspecific so as not to compromise himself straight away. They emanated from one of the managing director's two private secretaries, and they were corroborated by what he referred to as disturbing details. 'I have known Just for almost ten years,' Rose told me. 'I used to see him frequently at our monthly meetings at head office, I am in daily contact with him here,

and for several months I have noticed that
he is no longer himself. It's intuitive, a
combination of minute observations, but for
anyone who knows the man, the disparity is
striking. I say disparity; I am tempted to say
illness, but I don't dare go as far as that.
It's for you who are a specialist in this area
to enlighten me on these matters. You must
understand,' Rose insisted, 'that this matter
is one of the utmost gravity, for Just is one
of the cornerstones of our business plans in
France, as well as of our recovery programme. In Germany, they want to know
what has happened to him, and they want a
detailed report. Should this report be posi-
tive, we would all feel reassured, myself
most of all, for I have a deep affection for
the managing director and even feel
indebted to him.' Karl Rose was silent for a
moment. 'For this *special* assignment,' he
continued, 'I leave you to organise your
time in whichever way you please, and to
allow anything that can wait to wait. You

will probably need to forge a personal relationship with Just, on whatever pretext, so
that you can get a clearer idea of the
problem. Every Saturday afternoon, Monsieur Just goes along to the company golf
club so perhaps you could use this oppor-
tunity to make an approach.' When I asked
Rose if he thought it advisable for me to
meet the secretary who had spoken to him,
the deputy managing director hesitated at
first, but eventually agreed, assuring me that
he would warn her beforehand, though he
requested that I conduct my investigations
with all due delicacy, since this woman was
very attached to her boss. I asked for a day
to think things over before giving my
response. Rose consented graciously. As I
took my leave, I had the sense that I had
been very subtly manipulated. I ought to say
that I experienced this feeling after every
one of our meetings, for the man never
allowed what he really thought to emerge. I
told myself that there was probably some

mysterious power struggle being waged between the two directors. If that were the case, and they were pretty evenly matched, then I could not fail to get my fingers burned. Rose had told me too much, however, and to turn down this assignment would be to risk my becoming an embarrassment from his point of view. In the end, I forced myself to agree, resolving to conduct a discreet enquiry and provide a report that would be as non-committal as possible. Had I not been deeply curious about whatever secret machinations were afoot, and even had the fanciful feeling that I might nevertheless be able to control them, I would have made up an excuse to turn down the proposal.

The elder of Mathias Just's secretaries had a moment of panic on seeing me push open her office door. Without asking any questions, she agreed to the meeting I proposed at one of the smartest bars in town, in the heart of the commercial centre. She was an unmarried woman, fiftyish, elegant but spindly, always dressed in an austerely cut suit. Her name was Lynn Sanderson and she had retained the smooth and gently lilting accent of her English childhood. She spent the greater part of our discussion denying that there was the slightest problem to do with her boss, and regretting that she had spoken openly to Monsieur Rose about an anxiety that clearly had no real foundation. Monsieur Just, she kept on saying, as if this had been my question, was a man of the greatest probity, someone who was scrupulous in his moral behaviour, and who had the utmost respect for those around him. At the most, she admitted, like all of us surely, he sometimes went through difficult patches, brought on by worries that she described as personal. As she spoke these words, she could barely conceal her emotions. When I assured her that my role was first and foremost to help anyone who was in difficulty, and that my professional ethical code guaranteed the confidentiality of our conversation, she seemed within a hair's breadth of lowering her guard. Today I can gauge the hypocrisy of this declaration of ethical faith and how much the use of the word confidentiality had to do with my agreement with Karl Rose. Lynn Sanderson fell partially into the trap. Her voice breaking, she let herself be drawn into revealing one of her boss's personal worries: the fact that he had had just one child, which was stillborn, and that ever since he had experienced periods of great unhappiness. 'No one can shelter from misfortune,' she observed, her eyes looking vacantly around her. In that moment I think I grasped that there was some special bond that linked her and her managing director. Perhaps they had been lovers, perhaps each of them harboured a love for the other that could never be declared, or had she loved him secretly, in that tenacious way that certain women are capable of – but in that case why would she have gone to speak to Rose and risked betraying this relationship? I did not discover the answer that day. I thought it advisable not to press the point, but rather to deflect the secretary's mistrust by discussing interests we had in common, and to make a date for another meeting later on. We shared a love of music; she was a violinist in her spare time, and a well-informed music-lover too, particularly fond of Bach, Fauré, Franck and Schumann. Monsieur Just was also an amateur violinist. This man who was apparently so harsh on himself displayed the utmost sensitivity where music was concerned. 'But he no longer plays, nowadays,' she thought it worth adding.

A confidential letter, addressed to me at home, gave an account of Mathias Just's career at SC Farb. It bore Rose's forceful handwriting (*'For your information'*) at the top of a document that had been stamped in German: BOARD OF DIRECTORS (HAUPT-DIREKTION): NOT TO BE DISCLOSED UNDER ANY CIRCUMSTANCES. From it I discovered that Just had joined the firm at the age of twenty-five. He had worked originally as an engineer, then, after a training period at head office, he had risen gradually to become deputy production director, and eventually managing director, still within the French subsidiary. His supervision of the reorganisation work was covered in just a few lines which simply mentioned his acerbic style in negotiation, and two appearances in the media, which were described as 'precise and convincing'. One particular fact drew my attention: before he was appointed managing director, Just had for some years presided over a string quartet to which three other musicians from the firm belonged. The Farb Quartet (as it was called) had performed 'successfully' at the company's annual party. They had last played together eight years ago. Clipped to the managing director's curriculum vitae were two curious-looking pages comprising several rectangular bits of paper arranged one on top of the other, which had been photocopied. I have reproduced certain of these dated fragments just as they are, extending over the last two years; they provide proof of an evident policy of denouncing colleagues carried out within the firm:

12.IV, 17.IV, 21.V: Inexplicable lateness.

3.VI: Unwell at the board meeting, incapable of reading his notes, the excuse being a migraine behind the eyes.

4.VII: Withdrew to his office all morning, did not reply to the telephone. Sounds of water(?).

2.IX: Adjustment to his signature, simple repetition of his flourish (copy attached).

23.IX: Complaint addressed to the cleaning company about documents claimed to have been spirited away. An internal enquiry concludes there is no evidence. Withdraws complaint.

6.II: Arrives in car-park one hour before office opens, remains motionless in car throughout this time.

14.II: Hunting permit appears to have been sent to document shredder.

5.VI: Under influence of drink (likely, unconfirmed), eleven o'clock in the morning.

9.VIII: Lost his leather gloves. Mad panic. Strange behaviour.

2.XI: His two private telephones replaced. Suspects a listening device.

12.XII: Wants to take steps to change his name

(substituting Schlegel, matronymic, for Just).
Request eventually deemed unacceptable.

A leaf from a square-rule exercise book had been stapled to the last page. It provided an example of his handwriting. It was probably a message handed to Rose during a meeting. The words, which were barely legible (*'Karl, don't mention B. in your presentation, they know about him'*), had been crossed through in pencil with oblique lines, with circles around the letters *p* and *n*, and certain gaps in the middle of words had been underlined.

My visit to the golf club the following Saturday proved unproductive. I learned that he had not been to the place for several months, that he used to go there very regularly, and that he would play the same nine holes, sometimes when it was raining, by

17

himself. I resolved to try another angle of approach. Thanks to a friend, a woman who was employed in the personnel department, I got hold of some information about the Farb Quartet. I discovered that Lynn Sanderson had been a member of it, as were a sales representative, who had since been made redundant, and a chemistry graduate who played the cello, by the name of Jacques Paolini. The man received me amid his chilling world of screens, chromatographs and other precision instruments. He was a good-natured character, outwardly full of bonhomie, and with a keen sense of irony, even if he affected a languid tone of voice. 'Music is a capricious creature,' he told me. 'String quartets are trickier still. Take four cards: a king, a queen, a jack and a six. Or else: a king of spades, a ten of clubs, a six of diamonds and a three of hearts. It's a combination that can't work; it would be better to lay down your cards and miss your turn.' 'Who was the king?' I asked him. He smiled: 'You wouldn't have any difficulty guessing the four cards: a managing director – or almost one – a secretary, a sales representative, a chemist. Music does not like a hierarchy like that. Four jacks would have been preferable, or even four tens – now there's a pretty hand.' 'Was there any difference of opinion?' I ventured. 'No, not so much a difference of opinion,' he replied, 'as disharmony. We were not well tuned. The Franck Quartet was a disaster, and Schubert's Fourteenth not much better.' 'And how did Just play?' He was specific: 'With a tension, an obsessive exactitude, and with that penchant for mastery that puts music to flight. In all perfectionism there is an appalling fear of the void.' Paolini appraised me over the top of his spectacles. 'This experience has made you bitter,' I said to him. He evaded me tactfully: 'Bitterness is a condition, that's something I learned from my instrument. Accordion players rekindle people's melancholia, violinists attempt the sublime.' His face lit up with a shrewd smile. 'And you, what do you know about music, Mr Industrial Psychologist?'

My first contact with Mathias Just took place over the telephone the following day. He insisted on knowing the precise reason for the meeting I had requested. When I mentioned the Farb Quartet, he paused for so long that for a moment I thought we had been cut off. The interview was arranged for that same evening, at half-past six prompt, after the secretaries had left and the office was officially closed. In my memory, that first encounter is like an over-exposed film, something rather frightening. The strip lighting on the ceiling cast a very harsh glare, and Just stared at me, motionless; I can still see the hard look on his bony face, those bushy eyebrows, the crew-cut chestnut hair, the very large mouth and sturdy neck. He questioned me insistently about the reasons for my interest in the Farb Quartet, without once seeming satisfied with my replies. On several occasions, he jotted something down in a tiny notebook and he even made me spell out my name, although he must have known it perfectly well. The fact that I should wish to ascertain, within the framework of my responsibilities, whether the idea of an internal company chamber group could be revived struck him as peculiar. He suspected something else. Because my arrival at the firm had been subsequent to the disbanding of the quartet, he insisted absolutely on knowing who had told me about it. My reference to Paolini appeared to displease him, but he made no comment. Abruptly, he asked me to describe the nature of my seminars, which he said he mistrusted, but which were 'all the rage'. He stood up, rather suddenly, right in the middle of my explanation and went to wash his hands in the bathroom adjoining his office. From where I was sitting,

I could watch him from behind, scrubbing his hands methodically with a small nailbrush, and so immersed was he in this task that I had the impression he had forgotten me. When he returned and sat down again, he appeared to be relieved and at the same time absent-minded. He said: 'I shall look among my personal belongings to see if I still have a recording of what we used to do.' And he accompanied me to the door without offering to shake hands.

Very early the next day, he himself called me to say that he had found his file on the Farb Quartet, and that he would like to invite me to his home the following Saturday to hear more about it. He spoke in fits and starts, and between the pauses the flow of his voice was hurried. I thought he would cancel this invitation later on. He did not cancel it. If the truth be known, the prospect of this meeting slightly alarmed me, because I could foresee it speeding up the pace of a story that I had believed I was able to control. I also attributed my uneasiness to the rather funereal aura that this man imparted, to the extreme nervous tension that restricted his movements, and to the terseness of his remarks, as if the only thing he knew how to do when confronted by another person was to take orders or issue instructions. I choose the word funereal, remembering that he seemed to me to be preoccupied as much by death as by murder, and the very rapid shifts from rage to anxiety that his expression revealed made me hesitate between the two aspects of the impulse.

He lived in one of the recently constructed villas by the lake, a cold and luxuriously appointed house surrounded by a perfectly maintained garden in the French style. An electronic remote-control device operated the gate. The front door was set off by two unbleached marble columns on either side. He received me in a small smoking-room adjoining the hall. He looked ill at ease sitting in a squat armchair that was too small for him, among those middle-class surroundings of display cabinets, sets of china and pretty mahogany picture frames. But it was not merely his height, nor the suppressed violence that seemed out of place in the little room; there was something slovenly about his appearance, an unguarded, sometimes abrupt eye contact and a sort of off-hand manner that belied his anxious expression. I became aware that he was drunk. I even reckoned that he had been drinking to relieve the fear my visit had provoked, that he had had a premonition that I would bring up a subject which he could no longer evade and had realised that he would be forced to enter into a relationship with me. When his wife hurried in with a tray of glasses for our apéritif, a mere glance was enough for me to see how distressed the woman was. She was a small, neatly dressed woman, old before her time, with a white chignon crowning a face with sad eyes: from all appearances a submissive wife of the kind that is known in these circles as a homemaker. Her first name was Lucy. Once she had returned to the kitchen, we resumed our conversation. It proceeded in snatches, somewhat disjointedly, peppered with questions concerning my private life (but did he hear my answers?), general remarks about music, and memories – since these were what I had come for – rather strained memories to do with his learning the violin, with the setting up of the Farb Quartet and its rare moments of triumph. He had been taught by a certain Zoltan Nemeth, whose name it would have been in poor taste for me not to have known. The quartet used to rehearse on Tuesdays and

Sundays, his secretary had been a member of it, and they had tried their hand at Dvořák, Franck and even Schubert. Recalling this, he murmured in a subdued voice: '*Death and the Maiden*, I've found our recording.' And he stood up, a little shaky on his legs, and invited me to follow him to a spacious room, whose tall bay windows looked out over the lake. We sat down facing the window, surrounded by half a dozen loudspeakers placed around the room. He turned on the stereo by remote control and the first notes of the andante rose up, slow, too slow, discordant and a bit mechanical, but nevertheless full of that intense melancholy that suffuses the Viennese master's purest works. It was then that the incident occurred: initially I heard him utter some sounds in German, something muffled and vaguely incantatory, then he threw his head back and, gripping both armrests, began to shout: '*Genug! Genug!*' Finally, he turned off the machine. Having gradually recovered his composure, he repeated: 'It's unbearable, don't you see, unbearable,' and he added the following remark, which I later noted down, so curious did I find it: 'The music of the angels, you see, they have ganged up in tens, in twenties, to tear my body apart . . .' After which he continued to stare for a while, his hands clutching the armrests, then he got up abruptly and left me on my own. A door slammed somewhere in the house, and there was the noise of something tumbling down the stairs. Then Lucy appeared in the doorway.

Shaking and very pale, she murmured: 'It's nothing serious, my husband is a sensitive person and he hasn't listened to music for several months.' And she insisted that I should not leave without at least saying good-bye to her husband. He reappeared a few moments later, looking dazed but doing his best to smile, and trying to minimise what had happened. He put it down to the quartet's wretched performance and the terrible perfectionism that made him lose all 'common sense' when he realised the countless mistakes that he may have made. When we returned to the smoking-room, he was still out of breath, his eyes were gleaming and he was doing his best to pull himself together. Once Lucy had left us on our own, he asked me whether I had any regular contact with Karl Rose, anxious to know if the deputy managing director took an interest in my work and whether he felt concerned about my department. I evaded the question as best I could. Then he said these words: 'Your job interests me, the human question interests me, and I should like to talk to you about a specific problem, but later on.' I invented some family commitment in order to escape.

Lucy Just called me at the office on the following Monday. Her voice was trembling.

On a fairly flimsy pretext (I had forgotten my tobacco pouch), she invited me to call at her house again as soon as possible. I decided to call on her in the late afternoon, well before the time Just usually left the office. She ushered me into an enormous dining-room in which the silence was tightened by the metallic ticking of a clock on the wall. From the other side of the table, behind a tea tray which she did not touch, Lucy chose her words with care, scarcely daring to look up. 'I don't really know who you are or what your intentions are,' she began, 'but I trust you have thought carefully about what you are doing, and that your knowledge of psychology will allow you to understand without making judgements. As you yourself must have realised: my husband is not well. Listening to music was an unbearable ordeal for him, no doubt, but you couldn't have known this. Mathias has not been able to listen to music for a long time. He claims that it causes him pain, that it's like swords cutting

through his body – those are the sort of
things he says. But what terrifies me, Monsieur – and I want to find the right words – is
the expression on his face at certain times;
it's as if he could no longer control himself.
At night, he shuts himself away in his study
and I can hear him walking to and fro,
talking in a loud voice. I wanted to take away
the pistol he keeps because he sometimes
says the most dreadful things. But the gun is
no longer in its drawer. The other day I
caught him in our little Aloïs's bedroom. He
was lying down beside the cot – his big body,
can you imagine – and so I took him by the
hand and he just allowed himself to be led
away. The death of our child is a sorrow that
will never disappear, even though the poor
little creature never drew a single breath. Try
to understand, Monsieur, the hope that a
child represented in a house as large and
beautiful as this. On two occasions, we
thought of adopting, but each time, I never
did understand why, Mathias broke off

proceedings. I have reason to believe that he dislikes Monsieur Rose, and yet we used to get on very well with him. Madame Rose was a close friend of mine, but he forbade me to see her again. Perhaps I shouldn't be telling you all this, Monsieur, for I can imagine how upset he would be if he knew that I was confiding in you, but who else could I speak to? He refuses anyone else's help, he doesn't believe that he is ill, and he says that there's a conspiracy against him. The word frightens me, for in your field I think you call this paranoia, don't you? Unless there is some genuine conspiracy . . . but in that case why doesn't he speak to me about it? We used to be a very close couple, but nowadays even his study door is closed to me.' At last, she looked up at me. 'Can you help me to understand my husband?' she implored softly.

I did not know how to respond. I promised to keep in touch with her and to wait for the meeting that he had proposed before forming an opinion. These few words appeared to

comfort her. On the wall hung a large photo-
graph in which Mathias Just, looking stiff and
very solemn, could be seen standing beside
little Lucy, who was nestling against his
shoulder, a tender, cheerful expression in
her eyes that I had not seen before. In this
large mock-Gothic dining-room, with its
chandeliers and pewter candelabra, this
framed reflection of another age seemed to
portend unhappiness. Lucy shook my hand
anxiously and stood in the doorway until my
car had turned the corner of the street. She
looked as if she was still imploring help and,
with her slight body, was trying to conceal
the flickering shadow of the man with whom
she had shared expectations and cold nights
for so many years.

The packet that Karl Rose sent me, which
was also addressed to me privately, added a

new element whose true significance I was unable to grasp immediately. It contained a fairly long handwritten letter sent by Mathias Just to the managing director of the head office. The typed version was appended to it. It concerned an apparently commonplace technical document that referred to production figures, data concerning the staff, and forecasts and projections for the year ahead based upon two hypotheses, K and B, which were not specified. What Karl Rose wished to bring to my attention was not so much the content of the letter as the differences between the original handwritten version and the typed copy. The manuscript text was actually scattered with missing words that did appear in the final version. I concluded that Just's secretary, probably Lynn Sanderson, had corrected her boss's letters, but, once again, I failed to understand how she could have covered up for his mistakes and at the same time act as an informer. For me this question obscured the central element of this twin document. I did not realise that it was not simple error that was responsible for the omission of words, but that the missing nouns belonged to a group of terms with particular meanings, that they were like pieces of a rebus to which neither Rose nor I held the key. It was later, rereading the letter, that I would notice the omission of certain words such as *Abänderung* (modification), *Anweisung* (instruction) or even, on two occasions, *Betrieb* (functioning). In Just's mind, therefore, there was a censoring of words, like a computer virus that blocked certain terms and produced an empty space, a blank. Had I had the presence of mind at the time to put these missing words together, as if they belonged to some proscribed, but secretly used language, I might perhaps have solved a part of the enigma. A careful reading would even have helped me discover certain slips of the pen or the presence of an illegible intruding word, *Reinigung* (cleaning) or *Reizung* (stimulation) . . . It was the badly written and the badly expressed, the curse running through this entire story, which was jumbled together in the original version of this technical letter, with its rushed, panic-stricken handwriting, as if the smooth thread of what he had called common sense had been contorted and was beset on all sides by the rising tide of tumult, insanity, the unmentionable.

'The human question, the human question,' he reiterated. I can see him on that evening of our third meeting and I can remember that I felt physically frightened. He had called me in the late afternoon to arrange a meeting in his office punctually at eight o'clock. I did not understand what he was driving at with this 'human question'. It was certainly a reference to the way he perceived my job, but why did he lay such stress upon it? On this occasion he seemed to be in full possession of his faculties, even though his expression was tense and staring, and his tone of voice rather theatrical, as if he were rehearsing lines he had learned by heart. Once again I could detect an intense violence behind his solemn manner of addressing me. I feared that at any moment his composure would crack and that he would explode into shouting and abuse. As he talked, he ran his finger along a metal ruler that lay on his desk. 'I cannot ignore,' he declared, 'the importance of the human dimension; for me it remains a constant concern, and it is for this reason that I have insisted that you should participate personally in all meetings that involve the basic choices facing the company. And if, throughout the long ordeal that our restructuring has been for us, I have asked you to perfect and redefine our criteria for evaluating staff, it is because I have always been careful to take the human factor into

account along with our economic require-
ments. Even at our most critical moments,
you should know that I have never failed to
recognise the importance of this crucial
question. Any company, from the workers to
the managing director, has to confront this
issue sooner or later. From the workers up
to the managing director,' he stressed. Then
he paused for a long time; I could see his
mouth contort, and as a flicker of fear
passed over his face, I heard him declare in
a sombre voice, weighing out every syllable:
'I know very well, Monsieur, I know very well
that it is Karl Rose who has instructed you to
observe me. Karl Rose has entrusted you
with this task because little by little, by
spreading untrue rumours and by turning
my own colleagues against me, he is attempt-
ing to undermine me. If he wants to get rid
of me, it is because he knows that I have at
my disposal some secret and compromising
information concerning him, of an
extremely serious nature. The information is

the following, Monsieur, since at this stage I
no longer have anything to conceal: Karl
Rose's name is, or rather was, Karl Kraus. In
1936, Heinrich Himmler founded the movement known as *Lebensborn* – literally, the well
spring of life – with the purpose of gather-
ing together, from homes and maternity
wards, children of the Aryan race, often
orphans. By the end of the war, many of
these children were dead, but some were
adopted by German families, and this was
what happened to Karl Rose. The man is
therefore a Lebensborn child, something for
which he of course is not responsible, but it
explains why he should have grown up in a
family that was nostalgic for the Schwarzen
Orden and why he should have maintained
questionable friendships with people who
professed that ideology. I possess concrete
proof demonstrating that gifts approved by
him were made to a fictitious company
whose task was to transfer these sums to a
tiny far-right group, within which there is a

paramilitary militia. All these documents are in my possession, Monsieur, for I also have my informers. And it has not been difficult for me to trace the network.' He gave a tense, almost forced smile. 'Do you understand now?' he said insistently. 'Do you understand?' And in the interminable silence that ensued – a long, hypnotic, mutual scrutiny – during which I could hear him mumbling silently to himself, I thought I caught the word *Todesengel*, which means angel of death. He stopped himself with an irritated gesture, swung his chair round in the direction of the window, and dismissed me with these words: 'For the time being you must do as you please, Monsieur. I have said what I had to say to you.'

Christmas was approaching. I used a bout of flu as my excuse for not appearing at the office for two weeks. Throughout the whole of this period, I heard nothing from Karl Rose. He had asked me for my report on Just by the end of the year. I was unable to write a single word. Even to have ascribed this simply to pressure of work would have provided a formidable weapon and I had no wish to serve a master whose intentions struck me as less and less clear-cut. Although I could not ignore the fact that Mathias Just was going mad, that his defences were collapsing one after the other, and that his allegations concerning Karl Rose were probably attributable to delirium, they had raised a doubt in my mind and made me feel I was participating in a morbid game in which I did not know the rules. And I could not rid myself of the idea that there was a grain of truth in Just's lunatic convictions. So affected was I that I found myself unable to complete what was a fairly routine recruitment dossier. It was the first time that I had recoiled from, and even felt a distaste for my work, something akin to the symptoms of a profound scepticism that I had never wanted to admit to myself. That period over Christmas turned out to be more dismal than ever. The streets were dripping with bright fairy lights, the loudspeakers broadcast schmaltzy orchestral music, and people piled into the shops in search of trivial objects in an atmosphere of humdrum celebration and endless consumption. During this time I was the target for a number of voiceless telephone calls in which I could detect the sound of someone breathing before the caller cut off with a dull click. Someone was trying to get in touch with me and was unable to speak. I don't know why I was convinced that the person was a woman. Perhaps this was confirmed to me when, on another occasion, I heard Lynn Sanderson's high-pitched voice on the other end of the line. She wanted to meet me, but a few hours later she cancelled our arrangement. I made up my mind not to speculate about this sudden change of plan, nor, indeed, to wonder about certain warning signs that I could not fail to detect. I preferred to remain in a vague state of uncertainty and to allow things to happen, if they were going to happen, as far away from me as possible.

Mathias Just's accident occurred on the 21st of December, the day after our third meeting. I learned about it through a letter that Lucy Just sent me a fortnight after the event. She wrote: '*I venture to write to you knowing that you are the only person to whom I have mentioned my husband's problems. In our misfortune, this terrible accident has had the benefit of forcing Mathias to allow himself to be looked after. He is now in the care of the hospital at R. After two very difficult weeks, I believe he is on the road to recovery at last. Yesterday I think I understood him to say that he would like you to visit him. I am acting as his messenger even though the signs he has been giving me are tenuous and possibly*

contradictory. Visiting hours are in the evening. I leave the house every day at about three o'clock to go to the clinic. Be so kind as not to mention even the existence of this letter to anyone. May God help you to understand him. Lucy Just.'

At the hospital in R., Mathias Just had been put in the psychopathology ward. Lucy was waiting for me by the door of his room. Immediately she said to me: 'He's never been as bad as this, I was wrong to make you come.' A dim light on the wall cast a yellowish glow around the room. Just was lying stretched out, his eyes closed and his arms alongside his body. Lucy bent down to whisper in his ear that I was there. He did not react. His rapid breathing indicated that he was not asleep and that he was in fact fully aware of the slightest noise, protected as he was behind that cloak of rigidity that is known as catatonia. I mumbled a few words; in the silence his lips moved and I could hear him mutter: '*Schmutz, Schmutz*', which means dirt, stain, or filth. I laid my hand on the edge of the bed and felt him shifting his own hand towards my arm. Then he suddenly gripped it with such strength that it was as if my entire mind were held captive by this powerful, heavy, almost painful pressure. It was a moment of enforced intimacy with this man who I knew had a phobia about physical contact. Unable to move, I scrutinised his bony profile, the slow trickle of his drip-feed and the small notebook on his bedside table, in which a few words had been jotted down in unsteady handwriting. After a long while his grip slackened and I had the impression that he had fallen asleep. Lucy accompanied me to the hospital entrance. She then told me the true version of the accident. It had been a Tuesday, and he had waited for her to set off to her choir practice before driving his car into the garage. There, using wide strips of adhesive tape, he had methodically sealed off every air inlet, then he had taken some sleeping tablets, started the engine and, having opened the car windows, had fallen asleep in the passenger seat. His life was only saved thanks to a premonition Lucy had had in the middle of her rehearsal. She described to me in fascinated detail all she had had to do to force her way through the suffocating exhaust to reach the car, switch off the engine, drag her husband's body as far as the stairs to the laundry-room, and manage to unblock the mechanism that opened the garage door. After he had woken up, she told me, he began uttering terrible words. She went into detail: they were words of negation, dark, despairing visions – the notion that all the children in the world were dying one after another, and that there was some sort of damnation that would weigh upon mankind for evermore. Lucy had difficulty saying these words, as if they were forbidden or blasphemous. I wanted to know whether her husband had shown any such symptoms following the death of little Aloïs. She paused for some time and then replied with something quite unrelated. Later, I understood the relevance of this seemingly inappropriate answer. She described his father, Theodor Just, a shopkeeper who had been badly affected by the war, a brutal and unbending creature who knew only one word, '*Arbeit*', and who, if his only son did not succeed perfectly in carrying out whatever he was doing, would inflict extreme punishments on him, such as beating him with a leather strap until he bled or shutting him up in a cellar without lights for a whole day. Just as I was about to leave, Lucy asked me to stay with her a little while longer. In silence, we walked along the pathway that enclosed a patio. 'Don't leave us alone,' she begged me, before saying goodbye, 'I know how much he needs you.' It was bucketing down that evening.

Driving home in the pelting rain, I had the
very clear sense that I had penetrated a
man's inner darkness; worse: that his darkness impinged on my own and that the way in
which he laid his hand on me had been like a
seal of complicity, like a shared transgression
– the sheer pleasure of that sharing having
something sombre and indistinct about it,
strangely linked in my mind to what he had
called the human question. This sequence of
associations returned at night, bringing endless wakefulness and bouts of restlessness
staked out by the red figures of the digital
clock, while the same images would process
past and gradually peter out, until the pale
light of dawn eventually left my body
exhausted and numb with tiredness.

Karl Rose sent this peculiarly hypocritical
note inviting me to get in touch with him

again: '*I was shattered to hear of M. Just's accident. Fortunately, the news that his wife occasionally gives me is reassuring. I should be glad to discuss with you the matter we spoke of before, even if this very sudden event appears to have somewhat altered the hand to be played.*' The meeting took place two days later. I could soon see that Rose had not been informed about the real cause of the accident and that he was desperate to learn more. He must have been aware that I was feigning ignorance. He chose another line of attack: how did I think Mathias Just had looked? I was evasive, I lied about our encounters, but he forced me back against the wall and wanted to know what I meant by the obvious tiredness, by this personal crisis 'that all of us go through'. He watched me as I corrected myself, retracted, qualified what I had said previously, changed my mind and made out that I knew virtually nothing, before I finally conceded that the task with which he had entrusted me had driven me into a state of deep uneasiness.

This confession gave rise to further questions. Wild with curiosity, all his senses sharpened, Rose watched out for inconsistencies, ready to pounce. At one moment I seemed to see the word LEBENSBORN loom up in huge letters and I felt as if I were looking at him in the same way Just himself had done: as Karl Kraus, a child of the Schwarzen Orden movement, as a child who belonged to nobody, a child belonging to another variety of children, all perfect and similar-looking, a child without a childhood, without heart, soul, or descendants, a child of the pure new technical generation, the Source of life. Finally, he retreated: 'I do not understand your unease,' he said, 'and in any case you're not explaining it to me. You claim that a personal crisis is an inevitable transition in a man's life, which is either a generalisation, a smoke screen, or else a deliberate move beyond the scope of our discussion.' And he ended with these scornful words: 'I think I have made a mistake in consulting you, Monsieur, just as I have overestimated the advances in knowledge that your profession has made.' The meeting was concluded in silence and with an icy handshake. I went back to my office, but I was unable to concentrate on my work. I gave the excuse of a migraine and returned home.

It was the 10th of January when Lynn Sanderson called me in the evening. She wanted to see me urgently, but was uncertain about where to meet and preferred that it should not be somewhere public. We met at her flat, an enormous sunny penthouse that had been exquisitely decorated: pastel-coloured walls, hung with a few hunting scenes and some Italian landscapes, and floral patterned curtains. Here I saw her as the person she really was, a hunted woman, racked by remorse, whose veneer of elegance was cracking all over. For over a year, she confessed to me, she had been subjected to pressures and blackmail, which had led her to betray her boss, sometimes because of fear of reprisals taken by the Germans (as she referred to Karl Rose's colleagues), or sometimes because of the alarming state that Mathias Just was in. Almost abruptly, she admitted that she had been her boss's mistress, especially at the time of the quartet. The relationship had later become strained, due to Mathias Just's violent, unpredictable behaviour. That she had loved this man, that she still loved him, was obvious from the hoarse timbre of her voice and the cautious way she spoke of him. But the time had come for her to confess everything to me, to tell me all. She poured another drink and the alcohol relieved her of a secret that she had repressed for too long. I was privy even to intimate, almost indecent details of their relationship. He drove her back home after the quartet's rehearsals, he addressed 'poetic' love letters to her, he was a restless lover, possessive and obsessed by the fact that they might be caught unawares. According to her, his unhappiness dated back to two years previously, but it must have been smouldering for much longer. In private, this man who was so tough, demanding and unbending, turned out to be profoundly vulnerable, a child beneath an apparently seamless social carapace. On several occasions she had seen him convulsed with tears, unable to explain what prompted these fits of despair. It was this inconsolable child whom she had grown fond of, despite his violent rejections, his long periods of silence, and the awkwardness of a love affair built on rare moments of mutual understanding against a backdrop of pain and incomprehension. At the end of the evening, she recounted one of Mathias Just's childhood memories. I shall describe it in detail because it seemed to me, just as it did to her when she was relating it, to lie at the heart of this man's suffering. It's the sort of thing that leads one to believe in that kind of causality that makes of a single occurrence the basis from which everything appears to originate. During the war, Mathias' father, Theodor, had belonged to a police battalion which assisted the SS in so-called occupation duties in Poland and in Byelorussia. These duties were not purely administrative since they involved carrying out an entire 'resettling' programme in a region that was well populated with Jews. Mathias never knew exactly what his father's job was, but he did witness one particular incident. One Sunday, during the early 1950s, someone recognised his father in a museum gallery. The man had a limp, and there was a gleam in his eyes. He approached Theodor Just and spoke to him. Mathias' father pretended not to hear what the child would remember only too clearly: 'I saw you at Miedzyrzec in October 1942,' the man said to him. 'There were women and children lying near the cemetery wall.'

Without further ado, Theodor Just grabbed
his son by the arm and quickly left the
premises. At home, he raged about like a
madman and shut himself up in his bedroom. The following day, the man was waiting as he came out of school; he approached
Mathias and handed him a note addressed to
his father. On the note there was nothing but
a place name and some figures: '*Miedzyrzec
88-13*'. The father grew pale when he read
the note, seized his son by the collar, and
almost strangled him. Later, behind the door
to the cellar in which he had locked him up,
he shouted at him and threatened to kill
him. One day, he burst into the bathroom
and thrust the boy's head under the water.
'You should not have lived,' he yelled. 'Others should have lived, not you.' For a long
time, an image of his father looming over the
walls of the cemetery at Miedzyrzec haunted
the boy, and he wondered what the bodies
were doing lying face down against the earth,
and what the figures meant. He looked up

the place on the map and made up a story
for himself in which he imagined 88 to be
the number of women, and 13 the number of
children. Or else 13 was the number of children to have died out of a total of 88. He
thought that indeed he ought never to have
lived when these children were lying there in
the shadow of his father, who walked over
them in the same way that he strode across
the countryside, or paced up and down in his
bedroom like a lion in a cage. It was Mathias'
secret, Lynn Sanderson acknowledged sadly.
And she stood up in order to remove from a
chest of drawers an object wrapped in a silk
handkerchief that she placed carefully on a
coffee table. The almost ceremonial way in
which she set down the object, which
appeared to be a revolver, created a sudden
silence between us. But instead of thinking
about what Lynn had described, or dwelling
on the fact that he had given her the power
to prevent him from killing himself, I could
hear Lucy Just voicing her alarm at not find-

ing the handgun at the bottom of the drawer. I realised that by confiding in Lynn rather than in Lucy, he was placing his life in the hands of his mistress rather than of his wife. I was suddenly aware of the similarity between the two women: the same expression of anxious pity that could be seen in their eyes, the same doting, motherly affection. And they no doubt shared a physical resemblance, in their fragility, their slenderness, their delicate features: two sensitive, feminine creatures with whom he had fallen in love. I did not take the revolver (a Luger, the butt of which was inscribed in Gothic letters with the slogan '*Blut und Ehre*'), and I refused to touch it, even though Lynn twice expressed the wish that I should relieve her of the morbid bond that it symbolised. Before I left, I told her to throw the weapon away, anywhere, in the gutter, or in the dustbin. How I longed to be rid of this whole inquiry, to feel that it had nothing to do with me, that it was all finished, forgiven (but why this word forgive?), dismissed and closed, for good.

I resumed my work at SC Farb. Mathias Just was transferred to a multi-wing hospital 30 kilometres from the town. I got back to my recruitment and my seminars. Lucy Just sent me two letters which I did not answer. There was recruitment in the mornings, and on certain afternoons meetings, psychometric examinations and discussion groups consisting of eight to fifteen young executives, mainly sales managers. '*Mathias is gradually starting to talk again,*' wrote Lucy Just. '*He spoke to me about you.*' Occasionally I would suggest a break, and I would leave the conference room and smoke a cigarette; as I looked out of the window at the low, grey winter sky, heavy with rain, I saw myself as the elderly teacher I was, brooding over these concepts of motivation, assertiveness and selective skills without particularly believing in them, and advocating role play that always elicited the same comments and aroused a few credulous glimmers in the eyes of the participants. '*Mathias is talking more and more openly,*' Lucy Just wrote. '*Yesterday we went for a long walk in the grounds.*' I avoided Karl Rose and Karl Rose avoided me. If by chance he happened to find himself in my block, we would greet one another fleetingly, avoiding each other's gaze. Mathias Just's door remained permanently closed. I discovered that Lynn Sanderson had been on sick leave for three weeks. '*Don't desert my husband,*' Lucy implored, '*I know that you mean a great deal to him.*'

In mid-February, he rang me. I did not recognise his voice on the telephone immediately. It was slow and monotone, and slightly metallic, even though he told me he was feeling better, and that he had become aware of certain things that he wanted to speak to me about, if possible while Lucy was away. I could not ignore this appeal. My visit to the hospital took place on the following Saturday. It was a superb winter's day, crisp and cold, and the sky was deep blue. The various wards were scattered over extensive grounds and laid out around a nineteenth-century manor house. I was taken to the third floor of the old building, which was known as the Château. The door was ajar. Tinted glasses masked his face, and he was sitting in an armchair watching a television set with the sound turned off. He scarcely stirred to greet me, but he asked the nurse to close the door and to leave us alone. His speech was interspersed with long silences that seemed not to signify anything other than the time he needed to gather his thoughts. 'I am glad you are here,' he told me; 'I could not entrust this task to Lucy, and apart from you I don't see who could carry it out.' What he required me to do was to empty the safe in his study. To this end he had placed a small key on his bedside table together with a note on which was written a four-figure code. When I asked him whether I should bring him the valuable items from the safe, he replied almost irritably: 'There are no valuable items, they're worthless – *Unsinn* – do what you will with them.' He gave me no other information except to say that by doing this he intended to wipe the slate clean of a past that had been 'disgusting and hateful'; those were the words he used. He removed his glasses for a moment and I could see the dark shadows beneath his eyes, which were bulging slightly because of the neuroleptic drugs. With his old grey flannel suit, his shirt buttoned at the collar without a tie, and that look of stupefied stress in his expression, this man I was looking at was a shadow of my former managing director, a survivor, a ghost, a madman. He seemed in a hurry for me to leave and, urging me once more not to lose the key or the code, he muttered something like: 'You will see, Monsieur, you will see just how far human wickedness can go.'

There was nothing for me to explain to Lucy. She knew. She had accepted the fact that he would exclude her from certain things, just as she had probably been obliged to consent to his relationship with Lynn Sanderson. She scarcely bothered to ask a few questions (How had I found him? Had he been pleased to see me?) before she opened the door to his study and left me there on my own. There was hardly anything in this large room with its pale fitted carpet apart from two leather armchairs, a huge carved oak desk, a lectern made of the same wood, and an antique eighteenth-century music-box upon which five figurines of musicians and dancers, looking pale and bewildered, were arranged around a miniature harpsichord, each of them ready to spring into motion the moment the mechanism was engaged. In spite of the high windows that looked out over the lake, and perhaps because of the smell (slightly – exquisitely – fetid), I had the feeling that I was trespassing behind sinister closed doors, or even desecrating a dead man's room. The safe, which was also enclosed behind an oak moulding, was set into the wall. All it contained was a cardboard folder in which there were five letters. I stuffed them into my pocket, returned the keys to Lucy, and left hurriedly.

It is at this point that the story takes on a quite different aspect. A sense of terror – that Latin word *pavor* – comes over me when

I have to describe the letters that he had
kept in his safe and had not dared destroy. I
thought I had fully grasped Mathias Just's
secret, but I had only touched on that part
of it which was visible, which appeared to
concern himself alone, and which was
explained by his painful memories and
could be put down to a specific diagnosis,
like case studies I had read about in books,
at university. Thus he became merely a pawn
in his own story, while I was left untouched
and unscathed, protected by the distance
assumed by the observer. 'Apart from you,'
he had told me, 'I don't see who could
undertake this task.' I would have refused, I
know, had I not been prompted by a kind of
wild curiosity, by the desire to find out
whether the safe actually did contain documents that incriminated Karl Rose, and by
the exhilaration of possessing them and,
through them, achieve an untouchable sta-
tus, for a part of me still wanted to believe
in the Lebensborn trail, which was too

strange and too unusual, I told myself, to be simply the product of delirium.

The five letters were anonymous and were posted from the town of N. every other month, normally on the 15th or 16th day. The first dated from over a year ago. It contained a facsimile of a secret memorandum, several pages long, and bearing the date 5 June 1942, that was rubber-stamped with the words SECRET: AFFAIRS OF STATE (GEHEIME REICHSSACHE!), and had to do with technical modifications to be made to the special vans that were used to go to Kulmhof and Chelmno. Historians of the Holocaust are familiar with this letter. '*Since December 1941,*' it read, '*ninety-seven thousand have been processed* (verarbeitet) *in exemplary fashion with three vehicles that have been shown to function efficiently. The explosion that occurred in*

Kulmhof must be considered as an isolated incident. It was due to a handling error. Special instructions have been sent to the administration departments concerned in order that such accidents can be avoided. These instructions (Anweisungen) *have improved the level of safety considerably.'* Seven paragraphs followed that enumerated the technical modifications to be made to the vehicles. I have translated them literally:

1) In order to make it possible to fill up quickly with CO while avoiding undue pressure, two 10 x 1 centimetre slits will be made at the top of the back wall. These slits will be fitted with easily removable valves and sheet-iron hoods in order to allow automatic regulation of pressure.

2) The normal capacity of the vehicles is nine to ten per square metre. But the large Saurer vans cannot be used to such capacity. It is not a question of overloading but of mobility over all types of terrain. It therefore appears necessary to reduce the loading area. This can be achieved by decreasing the superstructure by about one metre. Reducing the number of items (Stückzahl) as has been done up until now is not a solution, because more time would then be required for the operation since the cleared spaces would also have to be filled with CO. On the other hand, if the loading area is reduced but fully occupied, the running time is significantly shortened. It should be noted that in the course of a discussion with the production company it was pointed out that a reduction of the superstructure would lead to a shift of weight towards the front, which would risk overloading the front axle. In reality, a spontaneous adjustment occurs, owing to the fact that, when in operational mode, the cargo (Ladung) tends to move towards the back door, which is why the front axle is not affected by any overloading.

3) The pipe that connects the emission to the vehicle is liable to rust due to the fact that the inside has been corroded by the liquids that are discharged through it. To avoid this problem, it is advisable to reposition the filling nozzles in such a way that the introduction is from top to bottom.

4) In order for the vehicle to be easily cleaned, an opening will be cut in the middle of the floor, secured by a 20- to 30-centimetre watertight lid, also enabling fluid waste to drain away when in operation. To avoid any blockages, a filter will be inserted into the upper part of the pipe's elbow. More substantial filth (Schmutz) can be removed through the large opening at the time of cleaning. To this end, the floor of the vehicle will be tilted slightly.

5) Existing observation windows can be done away with since they are practically never used. In this way a significant saving can be made in the equipping of new vehicles.

6) It is advisable to ensure stronger protection for the lighting installation. The protecting grille should cover the lights at a high enough level to make it impossible for the glass to be damaged. Practical experience suggests that these lights should be removed since, it has been pointed out, they are hardly ever used. Experience shows, however, that when the doors are closed completely and it becomes dark, there is always a powerful surge of the cargo towards the door. The reason for this is that the loaded cargo (Ladegut) pushes towards the light when darkness occurs. This leads to difficulties when bolting the door. It has also been observed that the noise (Lärm) that ensues when the doors are closed is probably connected with the anxiety aroused by the darkness. It would seem appropriate therefore to switch on the lighting before and during the first minutes of the operation. This lighting is also useful for night-time work and for the cleaning of the vehicle.

7) To facilitate speedy unloading of the vehicles, a movable grate will be built into the floor. It will operate by means of wheels on a U-rail. The mechanism can be opened or closed by means of a small winch fitted underneath the vehicle. The company responsible for making these improvements has said it is unable to proceed for the time being because of lack of staff and materials. It will therefore be necessary to have them constructed by another company.

The final paragraph proposed that the technical modifications should only be carried out as and when the repairs were effected. An exception was allowed for ten Saurer vehicles, for which an order had already been issued. Since the company appointed to fit out the vehicles had indicated during the course of a working meeting that the structural modifications did not appear possible, it was suggested that the H. company be requested to equip at least one of the ten vehicles with the practical innovations proposed.

Finally, the document had been submitted for consideration and for a decision to Obersturmbannführer SS Walter Rauff. It was signed by hand:

I.A. (Im auftrag: by order of)
Just.

The second anonymous letter contained the same document, but the text, which was cramped and very black, was superimposed over another, fainter passage of text that occupied the entire width of the page and whose characters were reversed, as if seen in a mirror. This other, overlaid text turned out to be a fairly muddled jumble of entirely current technical memoranda, of the sort that might be sent from one department of SC Farb to another, and which consisted either of comments about a new product, or else of extracts from internal notes emanating indiscriminately from the production or personnel departments, or even from management. These fragments, which were too brief to be identified, were pieced together end to end in a totally random sequence. I could make no sense of this grafted text, other than that it may have been placed there as some sort of graphic background to offset the bolder characters in the technical memorandum of 5 June 1942. Beneath Just's signature, the sender had copied this aphorism:

> *'An original whose imitators are better is not one.'*
> *Karl Kraus*

In the third anonymous letter, the two texts

had been given the same typographical values, and the first document had been defaced by words that had been reversed and overlaid in the previous letter. Sometimes one word would be replaced by another, sometimes a section of text consisting of present-day technical terms would suddenly appear, the whole forming a compact lexical web whose chimera-like composition produced strange, rather incongruous associations. More alarming still than the feeling of bafflement it induced was the cunningly disordered way it had been composed. It was as if some virus or genetic defect had randomly pieced the two passages of text together, so as to produce a final version that was grammatically correct, but which made no sense, as if the anonymous sender had left everything to chance. It was this apparent absence of any intention that gave rise to feelings of persistent disquiet. Later, as I methodically copied the appended passages for my own use, I could make only one observation: the words belonged not so much to the techno-logical language of practical engineering (which the first of the texts had neverthe-less suggested) as to that of a certain vocabulary of leadership, a language used mostly by personnel and management departments rather than in the workplace or on the production line. The sender's one manifest intention was to have enlarged the handwritten signature *Just*.

The fourth letter struck me as the most cynical. Here, fragments of the first piece of text, loosely separated, torn and decon-structed, had been superimposed over a musical score, visible like a watermark and arranged in the same graphic layout as in the second letter. To play around with a musical score in this way, to organise the elements of such a text almost as if it were a game, seemed to me the most appalling thing to do. The emotion I felt prevented me at the time from seeing what was actually staring me in the face. I had in my hands, without my realising it, the message that would lead me to the identity of the sender.

The fifth letter contained the same pages of the document but these were virtually pristine, apart from the heading, 'Berlin, 5 June 1942', and the signature, which had again been enlarged, I.A. Just. In between these was a faint text in which just a few words stood out here and there in their original typeface: *instructions, security, functioning, cleaning, observation, loading, noise, night-work, equipping, evaluation.* On these almost blank pages, the sender had written by hand:

Not to listen

Not to see

Ceaselessly wash oneself clean of the human stain

Use appropriate words

Which do not stain

Compulsory transfer (Aussiedlung)

Restructuring (Umstrukturierung)

Reinstallation (Umsiedlung)

Conversion (Umstellung)

Delocalisation (Delokalisierung)

Selection (Selektion)

Evacuation (Evakuierung)

Technical redundancy (technische Entlassung)

Final solution of the question (Endlösung der Frage)

The death machine is in operation

☆

Once I had recovered from the initial shock of reading this, I grew more and more convinced that the five letters represented five deliberate phases of a devilishly conceived stratagem. The intention went beyond the scope of simply wishing to destabilise Mathias Just; the objective was more far-reaching and it no doubt concerned me just as it would any human being. The sender struck me moreover as someone who was well informed and of superior intelligence. He had taken the risk of writing by hand, which therefore meant that he did not feel he was in danger of being unmasked. I felt intuitively that it could not have anything to do with Karl Rose. The deputy managing director would never, it seemed to me, have had the necessary psychological or 'artistic' subtlety to develop this subject and, in any case, the two samples of handwriting that I possessed were not alike in any way. Rose's was cramped, nervous, distorted and barely legible; the other was broad, well-spaced and almost calligraphic.

Some research brought to light the remark by Karl Kraus, the Viennese pamphleteer who died in 1936, in a dictionary of quotations. It struck me at the time as plausible and even probable that the virtually homonymous Karl Rose/Karl Kraus had influenced Mathias Just's troubled psyche and coloured his suspicions. The dreadfully literal way in which those afflicted by psychosis often interpret the world is well known, but between Rose and Kraus there was more than a simple assonance: there was a twisting of meanings, a malignant transition from the mother language into another, foreign one.

On the pretext of asking Just what I should do with the letters kept in his safe, I paid a second visit to the multi-wing hospital. He received me in the same room, on the third floor of the Château. He was sitting on a painted wooden chair next to a television set that was switched off. Perhaps he had been waiting there for hours, staring at the corner of the wall from behind his tinted glasses. His hands were shaking violently and his knees were jerking uncontrollably with that type of artificially induced impatience produced by anti-psychotic medicines. 'I told you they were worthless,' he kept telling me. 'Pure lies. My father wasn't in Berlin at that time, he wasn't an engineer. My father was a simple Hamburg shopkeeper, who was forcibly recruited into a police battalion in Eastern Poland.' He was silent for a long time. 'It's a disgusting process,' he went on, 'I had nothing to do with it. You must rid me of all that.' When I showed him that the handwriting on the last letter did not correspond to that of Karl Rose, he sneered accusingly. 'Kraus,' he mumbled, 'Kraus is far too cunning to sign in his own hand.' Someone knocked softly at the door, a timid nurse who addressed him in a rather forced tone of voice: 'Monsieur Just, your medicine, Monsieur Just.' She placed a receptacle containing pills on his table and waited silently until he had swallowed them. After she had gone, we sat facing one another again. I could not see his eyes behind his tinted glasses, but I do not believe he was looking at anything; he was expressionless, and even my own presence no longer mattered to him. I thought of that technical letter that had been defaced initially with an insane passage of text, and had been absorbed bit by bit in a process of destruction in which a few terms – common words, prophetic commands: 'not to listen', 'not to see', 'the death machine is in operation' – had surfaced here and there.

I was unable to rid myself of these letters.

The more I leafed through them, the more their meaning seemed to drift away from me. The sense of a word, a sentence or an image depends on what the other person wants to say to you. Who was this other person, what did he want to say and why should I feel, almost without my realising it, that I was the person to whom his message was addressed? The night following my visit to the hospital, I had an experience that was totally decisive. It was a dream that I must relate with all the precision of which my memory is capable. I was in a disused factory, a vast, deserted chamber in which all that remained were the concrete bases upon which machines once stood. Some projectors suspended from a gantry illuminated a small wooden platform upon which four men in tails were playing a quartet by someone named Rosenberg or Rosenthal. Behind them was a huge double door that was barred by a metal strut. At one moment, muffled knocks could be heard that grew more and more violent and seemed to come from the door. One of the musicians eventually interrupted the music, stood up, put down his instrument and began manoeuvring the strut so as to open the door. I woke up at that precise moment. I was in an extremely distressed state. An idea, a question, was beginning to take shape in my mind. I looked for the letter in which the musical staves appeared as if in watermark, and I had confirmation of what I must have seen without being really aware of it: the staves were grouped in fours, and the passages came from the score of a string quartet. The few scarcely legible annotations of tempo certainly provided me with no clearer lead, but they were enough to tell me more or less everything.

Lynn Sanderson refused to see me. Her excuse was that she was exhausted, the after-effect of an attack of hepatitis that had left her very weak. On her doctor's advice she planned to go to her mother's home in England for a rest. Since I persisted, she said finally: 'If it's to talk about Mathias again, no, absolutely not. The whole business made me feel wretched, and I said too much, even to you. I said far too much.'

I got in touch with Jacques Paolini again. He received me in his laboratory, as he had done on the first occasion: the same gracious figure, with the same urbane manner of speaking and the mischievous smile. He greeted me warmly: 'And what good news does the industrial psychologist bring us?' I handed him one of the passages from the quartet that I had recopied by hand so as to extricate it from the superimposed text. 'Have you played this quartet?' I asked him.

He seemed a little surprised, but did not allow himself to be disconcerted, put on his glasses and began to hum softly. 'The extract is extremely short,' he remarked, 'but it must be the Franck, second movement. It's true, we did have a shot at it at the time, may the composer forgive us.' Paolini appraised me from over the top of his half-moon spectacles: 'But why this obsession with the Farb Quartet? Do you really want to stir up those old ghosts?' I gave him a complicated answer, which he did not appear to believe a single word of. He did, however, allow himself to be led back to the subject of his memories and he described the fourth member of the quartet, who had been an exceptional musician. His name was Arie Neumann, he had worked in the sales department and must have left the company at the time of the restructuring. 'He was a remarkable man, this Neumann,' reflected Paolini aloud. 'Compared to him we were pretty mediocre fiddlers.' The chemist continued talking in this way, without any

trace of suspicion, and accepting the fact
that he did not entirely understand what lay
behind my curiosity. At the end of the interview, and as if laying a final snare, I asked
him whether he had ever heard of Karl
Kraus. 'You're certainly making me play a
game of questions and answers,' he com-
mented, 'and I'm not too sure of your
motives.' But he could not resist telling me
the following story. Karl Kraus was so eloquent that anyone who was anyone in Vienna
hurried to his lectures. One day, during the
1930s, Kraus, who had never had any time
for the Nazis, heard a speech of Hitler's on
the radio and was convinced he was listening
to himself. He was astonished to recognise a
voice that used the same oratorical techniques for seducing, entrancing and whip-
ping up the crowds, one that seemed to
creep along and smoulder in order to cap-
ture its audience, and which then grew
gradually louder and bolder and would suddenly erupt into threats and incantations. So

strong was the resemblance that Kraus was convinced that the young corporal had attended his lectures and had spirited away his fieriness and his voice, which were now being reproduced on thousands of radio sets, those *Volksempfänger* that the Nazi movement distributed to homes to broadcast Hitler's slogans. 'This story of theft through mimicry is a frightening parable,' Paolini concluded. His enigmatic smile remained with me for a long time after our meeting.

I did some research on Arie Neumann. I came across a staff recruitment file, written in my predecessor's handwriting. It provided certain details of age, family and professional career. Arie had then been fifty-five years old, and he was the brother of Cyril Neumann, a celebrated pianist who is no longer alive today. Someone had jotted down on the file:

'Attractive, unusual, not a hard worker, poorly motivated, results unsatisfactory.' From year to year, his assessment ratings had become mixed up with other numerical information that reflected his turnover figures, which were in more or less constant decline. Before joining, Arie Neumann had tried his luck as a freelance musician, he had then been involved with a company that manufactured small stringed instruments and later with a specialist publishing house. On several occasions, notes of hotel expenses had been scribbled over with the same terse comment: *'Overvalued'*.

I dreamed about the quartet on three further occasions, which I noted down were the nights of the 24th of February, and the 2nd and 4th of March. Each time, the dream distorted the initial scene, excessively enlarging the metal door and reducing the size of the illuminated four-sided room where the musicians performed. Eventually they came to resemble mechanical puppets, or even the little automated figures that perched on the musical box in Just's study. Anticipatory dread made me interrupt the dream increasingly early. On the last occasion, I could not remember anything, I only knew that it had to do with that particular dream, not any other, and when I awoke I felt as if I were suffocating, my pyjamas were drenched in sweat and my heart was thumping loudly.

On the 8th of March I received a letter addressed to me at the firm and recognised the handwriting immediately. Although it provided a shocking confirmation of thoughts that had crossed my mind on several occasions, I could not believe my eyes.

My hands shook as I tore open the envelope. Inside were two pages covered with lengths of buff-coloured paper ribbon, of the kind used on telegrams in the old days, on which a continuous text was printed, without any punctuation. Here is a passage that I have extracted:

> *-it-appears-that-satisfactory-results-are-obtained-when-the-tests-are-carried-out-according-to-the-behaviour-observed-in-each-circumstance-but-this-implies-a-detection-of-relevant-variables-on-the-basis-of-the-only-clinical-study-of-concrete-working-situations-and-the-elaboration-of-specific-instruments-rather-than-resorting-to-standard-tools-any-element-unfit-for-work-shall-consequently-be-dealt-with-in-accordance-with-the-only-objective-criteria-in-the-same-way-that-a-diseased-limb-is-treated-these-items-should-be-remembered-one-age-two-absenteeism-three-adaptability-in-the-areas-of-competence-convertibility-without-omitting-the-*

_assessments-regularly-updated-it-should-be-
borne-in-mind-that-persons-who-are-deficient-
are-capable-of-transmitting-harm-to-those-who-
come-after-them-the-final-results-will-be-
evaluated-according-to-an-overall-grade-
combining-all-factors-and-selecting-the-
predictors-according-to-their-suitability-for-the-
intended-professional-duties-various-
procedures-for-a-priori-or-a-posteriori-
classification-have-enabled-the-singling-out-of-
homogeneous-groups-and-individuals-where-
the-biographical-predictors-have-proved-to-be-
particularly-useful_

The stories and events in which we may have
wished merely to play the part of eyewitnesses,
supporting actors or occasionally narrators,
eventually ensnare us with their net of evidence. My first instinct was to tear up the
letter, but I kept a grip on myself and resolved

to discover the source of this cleverly and intricately assembled text. Most of it consisted of very ordinary phrases taken from an occupational psychology manual. These fragments, which had been placed end to end, could be seen to be of a vague and general nature, even if I could not fail to recognise a specific reference to my own work, and indeed to my personal contribution at the time of the restructuring. Given the absence of any punctuation, fused as they were in the same body of text, certain phrases revealed a different provenance: they were based on the original text and seemed to push the logic of the former to the limit, being composed of terms which had been maliciously inserted and which tainted the overall sense, to the point that certain words of a technical yet familiar nature had now taken on a variety of possible meanings not previously suspected. I remember that I was unable to carry on analysing this passage, which was intended to hold out a crude and distorted mirror to me.

At the time I received the letter, it filled me with anger and fear. Anger and fear because from now on I had become the target for the anonymous plotter. The man had shifted his attention to me, he had repositioned his weapon and he was aiming at me like a sniper from the dark angle of some window. Of course, there was no mention of the sender's name; the letter had been posted, just like those addressed to Mathias Just, in the town of N.

Paolini, with whom I immediately got in touch again, made the excuse that he had too much work at the laboratory, but agreed ungraciously to a meeting during the midday break at the company's cafeteria. This reluctance was something new. If he chose this place, which was far too public and where there was a constant din, it was because he evidently wanted to restrict our conversation. I encountered a man who was distant and awkward, and who did his best to digress and behave evasively. In due course I showed him an extract from the anonymous letter and asked him whether it was he who had omitted to sign these missives and who was amusing himself by playing this dreadful game. He paused and read the passage attentively, then he looked up at me with an expression full of ulterior motives and uttered these words: 'So this story will never end.' To the question: had he seen Neumann since the last time we met? he answered neither yes nor no, but maintained an eloquent silence.

That afternoon, I felt unwell at work, the first of a series of dizzy spells which would henceforth affect the running of my seminars and gradually lead to a wavering in the quiet conviction that had earned me my reputation for technical thoroughness. I experienced a sudden sense of dual personality, I found myself hesitating over words whose meaning was suddenly unfamiliar to me, while the look on the faces of those present accentuated my discomfort and my mounting anxiety led to a bout of profuse perspiration, even a feeling of suffocation. With the help of a few ruses, I attempted as best I could to pull myself together, and the rest of the session passed in a strained atmosphere, with my feeling I had to watch every word I uttered. Eventually I came to dread these seminars, making the excuse of a hypothetical surfeit of recruitment work in order to postpone them, and I did my best to bolster my confidence by spending the evenings plunged into frequently arduous scientific reading. I was overcome with doubts and I had the feeling that my own choice of profession (that choice occupational psychology textbooks ramble on about so much) was based on a fundamental misunderstanding. What in fact was the point of motivating people towards a goal that really meant very little to them? At certain moments, which fortunately did not last, I even had the sense that a spell of some kind had been cast over me. At such moments I felt the urge to throw the anonymous letters in the fire. I did not do so, realising the futility of such a gesture and feeling in a confused sort of way that there was still more to be said, that each of these letters constituted evidence of some kind that had not yet been tapped, and that to burn them would not get rid of their frightening or malicious implications. On the 22nd of March I received a letter that I feared as much as I expected. In it I discovered the same pages covered with a buff-coloured ribbon, the same phrases taken from an occupational psychology textbook, except that here (and a comparison of the two letters left no doubt) the original technical text had been encroached upon and almost absorbed by the *other* text from which I have lifted the most significant passages:

-any-element-unsuited-to-work-shall-
consequently-be-dealt-with-in-accordance-with-
the-only-objective-criteria-in-the-same-way-that-
a-diseased-or-gangrenous-limb-is-treated-

-the-screening-shall-be-carried-out-according-
to-existing-plans-in-doubtful-cases-it-is-useful-
to-refer-to-the-questionnaire-of-the-
Reichsarbeitsgemeinschaft-Heil-und-
Pflegeanstalten-

-the-T4-programme-will-take-account-of-
the-capacity-of-the-mechanical-work-by-
this-is-meant-the-ability-to-practise-
efficient-movement-without-loss-of-
performance-

-at-Grafeneck-nine-thousand-eight-hundred-
and-thirty-nine-were-treated-at-Sonnenstein-
five-thousand-nine-hundred-and-forty-three-at-

FRANÇOIS EMMANUEL

*Bernburg-eight-thousand-six-hundred-and-
one-and-at-Hadamar-ten-thousand-and-
seventy-two-*

The reference here to the programme of
eradication of the mentally ill, christened T4
(*Tiergarten 4*) by the Nazis, struck me as
worse than crude: it was insulting. But this
time he had written his name on the back of
the envelope: '*Arie Neumann, Café Salzgitter,
N., evenings, between five and seven o'clock.*'

I shall always remember that large, sombre
café with its old-fashioned dancefloor and
ancient glossy white piano. Two waiters in
uniform were gliding in between the tables
amid a soft hubbub of voices and a background noise of distant music. The custom-
ers were whispering as if they did not wish
to disturb the atmosphere. It was some time

before I spotted him on the opposite side of the dancefloor, and it seemed to me that it could only be him: this man sitting alone at a table, an overcoat rolled up in a ball beside him, who was smoking in silence, a thoughtful look in his eyes, and from time to time jotting down something in a small notebook. A frayed sweater, long grey hair, gathered at the back in a black band, a face from which the bone structure protruded and which looked pale beneath the lights. The waiter approached him with respectful wariness as he replaced his glass. I went up to him and murmured his name softly, 'Arie Neumann?' He looked at me with a puzzled expression, asked me my name and invited me to sit down. I have transcribed as faithfully as possible what was said during our meeting, although I am still unsure about certain words he used. I remember that to begin with I was transfixed by the clarity of his gaze, a gaze that was less concerned with seeing through me than in trying to recognise me. 'Why have you come to see me?' he asked with a pleasant, almost kindly curiosity. I replied: 'The second letter you sent me was a provocation to meet.' 'You could have ignored it,' he argued in the same gentle, detached tone. 'You could just as easily have thrown it into the fire.' 'I probably needed to put a face to it,' I mumbled. And I heard myself add in a strangled voice, 'There's something cowardly about sending unsigned letters.' 'Cowardly,' he echoed. Then he explained softly: 'I believe each of those texts was signed, Monsieur, whether it bore a name, or whether one was implied by the provenance of the documents from which it was taken. All I did was to assemble the fragments, none of which were my work, which means that I am not solely responsible for the matter that brings you here.' 'That argument is a bit facile,' I retorted. 'You know better than I do how each of these pieces of text was selected, addressed and pieced cleverly together. What is perverse about it is not showing yourself in the light of day. It's not honest, it's not human to behave in this way.' He looked at me in silence. 'You are right,' he agreed. 'Those are the exact words: it is not human.' And he added in a low voice, 'My only connivance was to play around with the text as one would with shapes on a blank page.' 'A gratuitous play on the surname Just,' I suggested to him. 'And yet it's all there,' he went on, 'in the terrible coincidence of a homonym.' Then he said: 'A play on the name, one word for another, a resemblance, it's chances such as these that can make sense of the meaning.' And he fell silent again. I had the impression that we could go no further, and that he would continue to reply to each of my questions in the same incontrovertible tone of voice, with these generalised, vaguely ambiguous formulations. And yet I could detect a look of sadness in his expression and even a barely concealed look of pain, which disarmed the conflicting feelings of fear and fury that had prompted me to attend this meeting. 'I have witnessed Mathias Just's slow decline into madness,' I resumed. 'The madness was there from the start,' he muttered, 'it was there before him, well before him.' And he made this comment: 'I have also experienced Just's madness, but at the time it was frozen, like his heart.' He took out his pack of cigarettes and offered me one. 'When Mathias Just played music,' he continued thoughtfully, 'he was like an industrious, anxious child who has a fear of heights and is clinging to his instrument. All the tension that was inside this man was present at that moment. It was later, later on, when the music had finished, that I was able to assess his inability to see, and also another kind of blindness that was far worse, much more comprehensive, something like a malfunction of the language that was assimilated by creatures like Mathias Just with their frozen madness.' 'Was it necessary to awaken that madness?' I asked him. He replied, weighing each word: 'I returned blow for blow, with all the insidious violence that nobody ever intends doing to anyone else, do you follow?' Then, since I admitted that I had not understood, he began to relate a story, a sort of gloomy allegory that once again had to do with the technical note dated 5 June 1942, as if we were never to be done with it, as if we were condemned to read and reread it endlessly. 'Over there,' he began, 'there's a grey lorry that is passing through the town, it's an ordinary lorry, constructed in metal, that is heading for the mineshaft that lies two to three kilometres from the outlying houses. The driver and the security guard are not turning round to look through the window that enables them to monitor what is happening inside the rear compartment. They are tired, they still have ten more loads to carry out before nightfall, ten times they will have to cross the town in the most wretched conditions. Particularly since they are obliged to run the engine at full blast during the first moments of the transportation in order to drown those sorts of cries and strange jolts that are almost destabilising the vehicle. Fairly soon, fortunately, everything is quiet again and the transportation can still be accomplished on time, according to plan. You can see one, two, ten vans converging on the mineshaft. "Where are the vans going?" asks a child standing by the window. "They're going to the mine, they're doing their job." When dusk comes, the vehicles are lined up in the school yard and the drivers are passing a bottle of schnapps between themselves; they are exhausted, but glad to have completed a day that had begun, like all the others, much too early. The security guards, for their part, have finished their totting-up and hand their reports for the day to a supervising officer who claps them on the shoulder and jokes around with each of them. The officer thinks that if the weather continues to be mild, and there's no rain to bog down the vans, he will be able to complete his assignment by the end of the week. And his commanding officer, the Obersturmbann-führer, the one who has drawn up the order one hundred kilometres away, will congratulate himself on the good progress of the operations. Were you to ask each one of them what they are doing, they would tell you that everything was going as expected, with a slight delay perhaps in the planning; they would reply in that dead, neutral, technical language that has made of them a lorry driver, a security guard, an Unter-führer, a supervising officer, a technical manager, an Obersturmbannführer.' There was a distant smile on Arie Neumann's face. 'Do you understand better now?' I shook my head. I told him that I was weary with all these stories about extermination and the

Holocaust, and that as far as I was concerned their constant mention stemmed
ultimately from a morbid voyeurism.
Scarcely had I uttered this remark than it
seemed to me misplaced, and perhaps a bit
aggressive. 'Are you Jewish?' he asked me
after a while. I flinched and I heard myself
replying that my father was Jewish, but that
Jewishness was passed on, apparently, via the
mother. 'Jewishness via the mother,' he
repeated, as if he did not believe me, and
he drew his hand up towards my face. It was
a very strange moment, and for a few sec-
onds he continued to move his hand over
my face and trace his fingers over it, as if he
were trying to decipher it in a tactile way. I
felt deeply embarrassed and I must have
recoiled momentarily, as much because of
the intimate nature of this gesture (there
was something almost hieratic about it, as I
recall, devoid of any obvious intention other
than of fixing me with a kind of slow,
watchful and incredulous recognition) as

because of the reference to Jewishness which still reverberated with the hypocrisy of my own denial. He lit another cigarette and I could see that he was trembling. The story which he then recounted to me throws a different light on what had just occurred. His voice was choked with emotion, and as he spoke he stared at me with a crooked expression, as if he were looking through me at somebody else. He had to pause and break off on several occasions. 'I see a station,' he began again, 'I see people, numbed and dazed, descending from sealed wagons. Among these crazed-looking creatures staggering about on the platform, I see a dark, imperious prince, standing beside an ambulance with a red cross that has been put there for appearance. The man is a doctor, he is separating the weak, the old and the sick in the crowd from those who are fit for work. "*Links,*" he says, "*links, rechts, links,*" these are his only words. A boy of twelve or thirteen, whom he has directed to the left, is wrestling his way like a young devil among the green uniforms. He already seems sturdy for his age, and self-willed. The medical officer hesitates, he thinks of changing his mind, then he pulls himself together and yells: "I said '*links*', what I have said is said." That night he is unable to sleep and he goes into his sleeping son's bedroom. His child, he knows, looks like that young Jewish devil and it was the resemblance, he reckons, the resemblance to his own child that had made him feel confused earlier on. Then he gets into his son's bed and he hugs him so vigorously that the boy weeps with fright; he can feel his father against his back and he wants to cry out, but he doesn't dare; he pretends to be asleep; his body, the skin of his body, can sense his father's body and he will feel it there all his life like some brute shadow dragging him down with it, with those two little words endlessly echoing like some faltering litany: "*links, links, rechts, links...*".'

He stubbed out his cigarette and I noticed that he seemed to be crying. There in the dusk light of the Café Salzgitter, without any contraction on his face at all, I had the sense that he was far removed from everything and unreachable, and yet at the same time so close, and infinitely vulnerable. And his emotion won me over. Eventually, I asked him why he had told me this. He replied simply: 'It's our entire history.' 'Whose history?' I pressed him. 'Yours or mine?' He appeared not to hear me.

'Are you Jewish, too?'

He shook his head.

'And yet Arie is a Jewish name.'

'Arie is not the name my father gave me.'

He left very quickly, laying his hand on my shoulder as a sign of farewell. I have gone over our conversation again and again in

my memory, and in the jumble of impres-
sions I came to the conclusion that he must
have both feared and desired the meeting
as much as I did. I tried to recall the
moment when the mood of our discussion
had changed, and I reckoned it was fairly
early on, at the moment he began talking
about Just and music. Then I remembered
the way he had traced his hand over my
face, and I told myself that in doing this he
may have been trying to break down the
barriers that lay between us, to force his
way through abruptly, and to refute the
anonymous violence of the letters, as if to
say to me: 'It's not that I want to avoid you
or to destroy someone I do not know with
these letters.' I thought about those
enemies who no longer regard each other
as enemies, about lovers who meet again
and forbid each other to utter a word,
about my residual feelings of drained
anger, of profound relief. I felt relieved
because the man now had a face. And I

remembered my anxiety when Mathias Just's hand had grasped mine, that harrowing grip which this man's face had suddenly dispelled. For the one had led me to the other, and in the end perhaps each of them came to merge into and look like one another, what with their tall figures, their hard, bony masks, the dark burden of memory they each carried within themselves, and that intrusive way they focused their gaze.

He did not come back to the Salzgitter, and I never saw him again. The waiter could give me very little information. He used to come and write there, he told me, on the far side of the dancefloor; he would have a few beers and he would speak to no one, you would see him for several evenings at a stretch and then he would disappear for quite long periods.

He must have been a musician because he
sometimes asked for a poster for a concert
programme to be placed in the window. And
the young waiter showed me a dark-brown
poster advertising a string ensemble concert
on the 8th of April. I made a note of the
details and I left it at that.

On the 24th of March, Karl Rose asked me
to come to his office as soon as I arrived
for work. He wore his serious expression,
told me that he regretted being obliged to
take such painful measures, and handed me
my letter of dismissal. No reason was given
for the decision, and the only explanation
he would offer me was this: 'Some of your
colleagues must have observed a certain
amount of lapses that are incompatible with
the practice of your profession.' He gave no
details. The interview moved on very

quickly to the terms of my notice, which he
hoped I would not serve out. As we parted,
he added icily: 'Good luck.' I had an hour
in which to gather together my personal
belongings in a plastic bag, return the key
to my office and leave the building.
Through the window a secretary waved at
me from a distance; she had a handkerchief in her hand and I believe she was
crying. I also felt like crying, out of humili-
ation no doubt, but out of sadness too, the
sadness of small reversals. A March snow
was falling, a few spasmodic, melting flakes,
as on that November day when Rose had
summoned me to his office. Thus, framed
by these two snowy parentheses, the winter
drew to a close, a winter cursed by fogs and
showers. I took a long walk around the
town before returning home. In my flat,
where everything seemed astonishingly
quiet, I put away my belongings (handwritten notes, professional textbooks), and out
of a sense of irony I opened a bottle of

champagne, which I drank until I was drunk.

The concert on the 8th of April took place in an ancient baroque church shorn of its religious insignia, its walls and woodwork stripped bare. The audience was sparse and the nave of the church was freezing in spite of some gas-fired radiators. At the beginning of the programme they played *Fratres* by Arvo Pärt. The Estonian composer, we were reminded, had been inspired by a vision of a procession of monks endlessly walking in the flickering light of candles. He said he used very few components, just one or two voices, and three notes that were drawn out and modulated over and over again. When the musicians mounted the platform that served as a dais, I saw again the precise scene from my dream. Arie Neumann was the last to arrive, and he was holding his violin with the tips of his fingers. Although the others had sat down, he remained standing for a while, his gaze fixed in my direction. The moment was one of silent and shattering revelation for me. And when the first notes soared up against a continuous background of droning sound, I saw what I had been unable to visualise, what I had been unwilling to see: those images, suddenly only too transparent, of the opening of the metal door after the strut had been lifted, the dark mass of bodies, the heap of soft, tangled corpses, *Ladung, Ladegut,* beneath the yellow glare of the grille-covered lights, slipping down the slow tilt of the floor, revealing a hand or a leg here, a crushed face there, a twisted mouth streaked with blood, fingers clutching the fabric of some viscous undergarment, filthy with urine, vomit, blood, sweat, slaver, *Flüssig-keit,* and all these bodies, *Stücke,* tumbling limply one on top of the other, as the weight of the mass moves towards the pit, all these pliant corpses, still enmeshed and jumbled together, this one stretched out like a rag doll, another looking as if it were shaking with convulsive twitches, each of them being slowly freed from the heap as the load is displaced, *Gewichtsverlagerung*, each of them being gradually unravelled from this asphyxiating human embrace, such as this face that has turned blue and stuporous, and underneath the *dicker Schmutz*, the shit, and those little creatures nestling among the women's legs, the skeletal old men, and those little girls with sunken eyes, those naked boys covered with ecchymosis, all those creatures, *Stücke*, who had names, *Stücke*, that belonged to a language which more than any other is dedicated to a sacred passion for names, words and ceremonies, *Stücke*, Moses, Moshe, Amos, Hannah, Shemel, Shemuel, *Stücke*, my mother, my beloved, *Stücke*, Micha, Maïka, Magdalena, *Stücke*, *Stücke*, *Stücke*, each of these bodies gradually emerging from the muddy bosom of the mass to fall one after

the other, in pairs, in piles, into the dark hole
of the mineshaft, *Dunkel*, to be swallowed up
in a sea of buried bodies from which cries
and shouting arise, nine discordant violins,
three strident notes. Fratres. Blackness.

I have no other memories that relate to this
story. I know that one day Lucy Just left a
message requesting help on my answering
machine, but I did nothing about it. A few
months after my dismissal, I found a job in a
home for autistic children where I still work.
It's uncomfortable work, and badly paid, but
I have no wish to leave. There is a wild
beauty about children who have lost touch
with mankind. That is not what keeps me
here, however. Perhaps it is their expressions,
for they see everything, and they are fully
aware of all our subterfuges, artifices and
weaknesses. One of them is called Simon,

like me. Whenever he is overwhelmed by anxiety, he bangs his head against the wall until he bleeds. Then you need to go up to him gently and persuade him to calm down by holding him close to you without destroying the little mental assurance he has left. It is this uncertain struggle, this endless fight against shadows that has taught me much more than did all the years of my brilliant career with SC Farb. Sometimes I think of it as my private act of resistance to Tiergarten 4. And I believe I enjoy living now on the fringes of society.

With gratitude to the Fondation Auschwitz de Bruxelles, and to Marie-Christine Terlinden for the invaluable help she gave me over the translation of the technical note of 5 June 1942. My thanks, too, to Pascale Tison and Bernadette Sacré for the 'coincidences' which they placed in my path while I was working on this book.

The translator would also like to express his gratitude to Cati Patel for her help with the translation of the original German text of the technical note of 5 June 1942.